THE CHRISTMAS ORANGE

DON GILLMOR ☆ MARIE-LOUISE GAY

D1534405

Stoddart
Kids
TORONTO • NEW YORK

We acknowledge for their financial support of our publishing program the
Government of Canada through the Book Publishing Industry Development
Program (BPIDP), the Canada Council, and the Ontario Arts Council .

Published in Canada in 1998 by
Stoddart Kids,
a division of Stoddart Publishing Co. Limited
34 Lesmill Road
Toronto, Canada M3B 2T6
Tel (416) 445-3333 Fax (416) 445-5967
E-mail Customer.Service@ccmailgw.genpub.com

Published in the United States in 1999 by
Stoddart Kids,
a division of Stoddart Publishing Co. Limited
180 Varick Street, 9th Floor
New York, New York 14207
Toll free 1-800-805-1083
E-mail gdsinc@genpub.com

Distributed in Canada by
General Distribution Services
30 Lesmill Road
Toronto, Canada M3B 2T6
Tel (416) 445-3333 Fax (416) 445-5967
E-mail Customer.Service@ccmailgw.genpub.com

Distributed in the United States by
General Distribution Services
85 River Rock Drive, Suite 202
Buffalo, New York 14207
Toll free 1-800-805-1083
E-mail gdsinc@genpub.com

Canadian Cataloguing in Publication Data

Gillmor, Don
Christmas orange

ISBN 0-7737-3100-8 (bound)
ISBN 0-7737-6079-2 (pbk.)

I. Gay, Marie-Louise.   II. Title.

PS8563.I59C47 1999   jC813'.54   C98-930493-0
PZ7.G44Ch 1999

Printed and bound in Hong Kong by
Book Art Inc., Toronto

For Justine,
my Christmas Girl.
— D.G.

ANTON STINGLEY'S
birthday was December 25th — Christmas Day.
When he was very young,
he thought the whole town was celebrating his birthday.
Naturally, he thought he was pretty special.
When he found out everyone was really celebrating Christmas,
he didn't feel special at all.
So his parents bought him extra, *extra* presents each year,
presents for his birthday
and presents for Christmas.
Anton had a round head and more toys than anyone.

Before his sixth birthday, Anton went to see Santa Claus at a department store.

"And what would *you* like for Christmas Anton?" Santa asked.

Anton took out his list, which was sixteen pages long. "I want a rocket ship," he said. "Bright red, filled with Popsicles. A swimming pool, a dog that can sing . . ."

"Well," said Santa. "That should keep me pretty busy." He tried to put Anton down and move on to the next child.

". . . a gun that shoots apple juice, hockey skates, someone to do my homework . . ."

"That's a lot for one boy," Santa said, a bit wearily.

"I'm still on the first page," Anton said. "I also want a spy watch that takes pictures, a fire truck, two hundred cookies . . ."

Santa put Anton down and gestured to the next child. "Merry Christmas, Anton," he said.

"I'll leave you the list," Anton said, stuffing it into Santa's pocket. "My address is at the top. There's parking on the street."

Santa looked at the line of children. There were one hundred and twenty-two left to see.

On Christmas Eve, Anton dreamed of all his presents.
They danced in his head like sugar plums.

But when he woke up and went downstairs, there was just one small present from Santa under the tree. Anton opened it. Inside the box was an orange. *An orange!* There had to be some kind of mistake. Where was the guitar? Where was the *car*?

Maybe they didn't fit under the tree. Santa must have left them somewhere else. Anton searched the house. Nothing. He checked the garage. No sign. Maybe Santa had gotten the address wrong. He woke up the Blinketts next door and asked if they had six hundred presents addressed to him. They didn't. What was he going to do with an *orange*?

There was only one thing to do. Anton would sue Santa Claus.

It was Santa's *job* to deliver presents. Anyway, they'd had a deal — sort of — and Santa hadn't kept his end of the bargain. He would take Santa to court.

Anton went to see a lawyer named Wiley Studpustle. In Wiley's dark office there were books everywhere. A half-eaten peanut butter sandwich lay on the floor. Wiley Studpustle was the meanest lawyer in town. He ate peas with a knife. He never slept. He had a pet spider named Pumpkin.

"What do you want?" Studpustle asked in a voice that sounded like a steel door closing slowly.

"I want to sue Santa Claus," Anton answered.

"I see. And ah, who is this Santa Claus?"

Anton gasped. *"You don't know who Santa is? Everyone* knows Santa Claus."

"I work late most nights." Studpustle stared at Anton with eyes the color of mud.

"You know, *Christmas.*" Anton said. "Presents. Carols. Ho, ho, ho."

"He's not that annoying fat man in the red suit, is he?" Studpustle asked. "The one ringing that ridiculous bell in front of stores?"

"Yes, yes. That's *him!* He brings presents to children all over the world."

"And what did he bring you?"

"Well, he brought me an orange. But he didn't bring me what I *wanted,*" Anton said. "I wrote it down. Sixteen pages."

"You have this in *writing?*" Studpustle perked up.

"I gave Santa the original and kept this copy for my files." Anton handed the list to Wiley, who skimmed it and made small, clucking sounds with his tongue.

"He didn't give you a magic carpet?"

"No."

"Or a bicycle that turns into an airplane?"

"No."

"Or a chocolate mountain, twelve kittens, a fishing boat?"

"None of it."

"Well," said Wiley Studpustle with a smile that grew like a weed in the sunlight, "this sounds to me like a broken promise. We'll see Mr. Claus in court."

"You mean you'll take my case?" Anton asked.

"Ho, ho, ho," Wiley answered.

Judge Marion Oldengray looked around her courtroom. Santa was sitting down. He looked tired. Hundreds of children and their parents crowded the courtroom. The biggest newspaper in town, *The Daily Porridge*, had called this "The Trial of the Century."

"Your Honor," Wiley Studpustle said, turning to face the people, "like every child here, my client Anton Stingley, had the expectation of presents from a Mr. S. Claus on Christmas morning." Wiley stared accusingly at Santa, then produced the list. "My client had been promised two ponies, a leather jacket . . ."

"We get the idea," Judge Oldengray said. "Make your point, Mr. Studpustle."

"My point, Your Honor, is that my client did not receive any of these things. Mr. Claus failed to deliver. We are suing for breach of promise and we are asking for eleven million dollars." The people in the court gasped.

Santa looked at all the familiar faces. He recognized Bobby Frankfurter. He had brought him a pet monkey. And Mrs. Doofus, who had gotten a green dress. And there was Ned Flathead, who had that mean dog that barked at him every year. One of the reporters was wearing the cowboy hat Santa had given him.

Wiley adjusted his suspenders and said, "I would like to call Mr. Santa Claus to the stand." The crowd fell silent. Santa walked past Anton. His blue suit smelled of mothballs.

He sat heavily in the witness box.

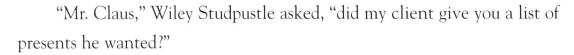

"Mr. Claus," Wiley Studpustle asked, "did my client give you a list of presents he wanted?"

"He did," Santa answered.

"And did you deliver any of these presents, Mr. Claus?" Wiley asked, his finger wagging near the tip of Santa's nose. "Did you deliver a *single one*?"

"I brought him an orange," Santa said. The crowd moaned.

"An orange," Wiley repeated. "No bike. No car. No hockey tickets. An orange. How thoughtful," he said meanly.

Wiley leaned close to Santa. "You are sometimes known as Father Christmas, aren't you?"

"Yes, I am," Santa replied.

"And Kris Kringle, Père Noël, Jolly Old Saint Nick?"

"Yes, all those names."

"I would suggest to you," Wiley said, "that you are neither jolly nor a saint. And your name *isn't even Nick!*" Wiley turned to the judge. "Would someone who is innocent need so many names? I think not."

The crowd went wild. Judge Oldengray banged her hammer. "Court is adjourned for lunch," she bellowed.

When Santa left the courtroom, reporters pressed around him, television cameras whirred. "Is it true, Mr. Claus," asked one reporter, sticking a microphone under Santa's nose, "that you brought yourself a brand new car this Christmas?"

"No," he sighed. "I drive a sleigh."

More questions filled the air. "Hey, Kringle, if that's your real name, how much money did you make last year?"

"How come you don't hire tall people?"

"Are your reindeer non-union?"

And so on. Santa's heart was filled with sadness.

After lunch it was Santa's turn to ask questions. He called Wiley Studpustle to the stand. Wiley approached the stand like winter closing in on a northern town.

"Mr. Studpustle," Santa began, "did you always want to be a lawyer?"

"Always." Wiley answered.

"There was never a moment when you wanted to become, say, a zookeeper?"

"Who wants to be a *zookeeper?*" Wiley sneered.

"I remember a little boy who wanted to be one," Santa said. "He loved animals. He was going to care for them and keep them safe. One Christmas, many years ago, I brought that boy a baby crocodile named Crunchy." Wiley began to sweat a bit. "That boy's name," Santa said, pausing for effect, "was Wiley Studpustle."

The crowd gasped.

Wiley suddenly remembered Crunchy and his adorable smile. His long-forgotten childhood came back to him and Wiley began to weep. "Oh, Crunchy," he cried, the tears staining his dark suit. "Oh, my Crunchy-Bunchy." He buried his face in his hands and sobbed quietly.

Santa turned to face the people in court. "You're unhappy that I didn't bring Anton Stingley what he wanted for Christmas. You're unhappy that I don't always bring you what you want. Well," he said, "it isn't my job to bring you what you want."

The crowd was shocked. There were cries of protest.

"My job," Santa continued, "is to bring you what you *need*." He looked down at Anton. "How many toys do you own, Anton?"

"I don't know," Anton said meekly. "Twenty?"

"In fact, Anton, you own eleven hundred and forty-one toys. Nine hundred of them have been played with exactly once. One hundred and twelve you haven't even touched. You didn't need six hundred new toys. Toys that would sit unplayed with, toys that could make other children happy. What you needed was something precious and small. You needed one perfect, mysterious orange."

The people in the court looked at Anton.

"For hundreds of years I've been doing this job," Santa said. "I have survived blizzards and budget cuts. I know who is naughty, I know who is nice. I know who dyes their hair blonde . . ."

"Yikes!" squeaked Mrs. Doofus.

". . . I've had reindeer problems, I've worked nights, I've never taken a holiday. I'm tired."

Santa looked tired. His eyes were heavy. His hair was white.

"And now you're unhappy," he said, looking at the people. "Well, I'm unhappy, too. I quit."

A silence descended on the room. A silence so big, so . . . *silent* you could have heard a mouse breath. Santa began to leave the courtroom.

"You can't quit!" someone in the crowd shouted. "You're *Santa Claus!*"

Santa stopped at the door. "I bring each of you a present every year," he said. "When was the last time any of you gave *me* a present?"

Ned Flathead stared at his shoes. "I meant to get you something," he mumbled.

"I was going to bake you some cookies," Mrs. Doofus explained. "I just didn't have the time."

Santa left the building and started down the courthouse steps. A murmur spread through the crowd, a murmur that became a hum that grew into a buzz. What had Anton *done*? What had *they* done?

Out on the street, Santa raised his hand to hail a taxi.

Anton knew he had to do something. He raced down the aisle and
hurtled through the door. "Santa!" he yelled. "Wait! Wait!" A taxi pulled up
and the door opened. Anton dashed down the steps. He didn't know what he
was going to say. He wanted to say that he was sorry he had taken Santa to
court. That he knew he had too many toys. He didn't want to be naughty.
He wanted to be nice. What did nice people *do*, he wondered.

They did nice things.

Anton wanted to give Santa a present. A perfect

and wonderful present.

In his pocket he felt something mysterious. He took it out

and looked at it.

It was as round as Anton's head and as perfect as the sun.

It was the Christmas orange.

He held it out to the tired old man who was getting into the taxi.

"It's for you," Anton said. "Merry Christmas, Santa."

"Where are you going, buddy?" the cab driver asked.

Santa took the orange and smiled.

"I'm going to the North Pole," he told the driver.

"I'm going back to work."